Karen's Reindeer

**Other books by
Ann M. Martin**

P. S. Longer Letter Later
(written with Paula Danziger)
Leo the Magnificat
Rachel Parker, Kindergarten Show-off
Eleven Kids, One Summer
Ma and Pa Dracula
Yours Turly, Shirley
Ten Kids, No Pets
With You and Without You
Me and Katie (the Pest)
Stage Fright
Inside Out
Bummer Summer

For older readers:

Missing Since Monday
Just a Summer Romance
Slam Book

THE BABY-SITTERS CLUB series
THE BABY-SITTERS CLUB mysteries
THE KIDS IN MS. COLMAN'S CLASS series
BABY-SITTERS LITTLE SISTER series
(see inside book covers for a complete listing)

Baby-Sitters Little Sister

Karen's Reindeer

Ann M. Martin

Illustrations by Susan Crocca Tang

A
LITTLE APPLE
PAPERBACK

SCHOLASTIC INC.
New York Toronto London Auckland Sydney
Mexico City New Delhi Hong Kong

ISBN 0-590-52454-2

12 11 10 9 8 7 6 5 4 3 2 1   9/9 0 1 2 3 4/0

Printed in the U.S.A.   40
First Scholastic printing, November 1999

The author gratefully acknowledges
Gabrielle Charbonnet
for her help
with this book.

Karen's Reindeer

December!

I sniffed. My nose felt chilly. But beneath the covers, the rest of me was cozy and warm. I wiggled my toes and decided it was time to open my eyes.

When I did, I saw that the sky was already light. So it was not too early. No one was calling me, so it was not too late. I smiled to myself. Everything was just right.

"Goody," I said softly. (I am usually very cheerful in the mornings. Not everyone is. You would be surprised.)

Throwing back the covers, I leaped out of bed and ran to the window. A thick blanket of fresh white snow lay on the lawn. It was a beautiful sight. "Yippee! Snow!"

Then I remembered something — something even better than waking up at the right moment, something even better than snow. I glanced at my calendar. Yes! Today was the first day of December! "Christmas is coming!" I sang.

In summer, I like summer. In spring and fall, I like spring and fall. But as nice as the other seasons are, the Christmas season is really my favorite time of year.

"Hello," I said to my bunny slippers as I put them on. (Wearing bunny slippers makes my feet feel cheerful.) Then I raced out of my room. As I dashed down the stairs, I thought of all the things I like about Christmas. I love the chilly air. I love making snow angels and snow people and having snowball fights. I love wreaths and holly and mistletoe and Christmas trees. I love

Christmas lights. I love caroling and baking cookies and making decorations. I love Santa Claus. And I love presents — shopping for them, wrapping them, and especially receiving them.

Then I stopped.

It was the first day of December. It was the first day of the Christmas season. And that meant it was the first day of Karen-on-her-best-behavior season too. (My name is Karen, in case you could not guess.) If I wanted to receive any gifts this year, I had to be as good as I could possibly be.

Now, I am normally a pretty good kid. Sometimes I have to be reminded to use my indoor voice. Sometimes my brother Andrew and I bicker a tiny bit. But I would say that usually I am somewhere between "very good" and "excellent."

In December, though, "very good" is not good enough. Even "excellent" might not be good enough. Because Santa has a list, and he checks it twice. He finds out who is naughty and who is nice. I needed to be extra-special gigundoly nicely excellently good both times he checked his list.

I took a deep breath. From this moment until Christmas morning, I had to remember to be perfect. All the time. Every single moment of every single day. Starting today.

This is how I behave every December — perfect all month long. And every year it works. Santa always brings me something great. One year I was so good, I got two great things (a talking doll and a paint set).

I turned around, went back upstairs, and made my bed. I even fluffed my pillows and put Moosie on top, like a decoration. (Moosie is my big-house stuffed cat. I will explain about the big house and the little house soon.)

In the bathroom I washed my face and combed my hair. I put the brush away neatly and hung the hand towel over its rack. I straightened the towel. There. Perfect.

I looked at myself in the mirror. Not a hair was out of place. Perfect again.

I was off to a good Christmas-season start.

2

Holidays Here and There

"Good morning, everybody!" I said in my indoor voice as I walked into the kitchen. My stepmother, Elizabeth, was at the kitchen counter. Sam and Charlie, my two older stepbrothers, were at the table eating.

I smiled cheerfully. "Mmm! That smells delicious! What is it?"

"Cereal," said Elizabeth. "Would you like a bowl?"

"Yes, please, I certainly would, thank you," I said. "I love cereal. It was kind of you to offer me some." I beamed at her.

6

Sam and Charlie looked at each other.

"What is with her?" Sam asked Charlie.

Charlie shrugged.

"It is the first day of December," Elizabeth said. "Christmas is coming."

"Ohh," Sam and Charlie said together. Then they snickered and went back to their cereal.

I just smiled at them. Even if they laughed at me, I would not say anything mean. Santa would be so impressed.

"Well, I am off," said Charlie. "See you all later." He started to get up from the bench where he was sitting. He picked up his cereal bowl.

I ran to him and took the bowl out of his hands. "I will take that to the sink," I said.

Charlie laughed. "Okay, Karen, if you insist."

"I do insist," I said. "I like to do favors for people." I said that extra loudly, in case Santa was listening.

As I walked to the sink with Charlie's bowl, I thought about how different breakfast was at my little house. But wait. I have not explained about the big house and the little house yet. I will do that now.

A long time ago, when I was little, I had one family and one house. The one family was Mommy, Daddy, Andrew, and me. (Andrew is my little brother. He is four going on five.) We lived here in the big house in Stoneybrook, Connecticut. Then Mommy and Daddy started arguing a lot. They told Andrew and me that they loved us, but they did not want to stay married anymore. So they got divorced.

Mommy, Andrew, and I moved to a little house not far away. Daddy stayed in the big house. (It is the house he grew up in.) Then Mommy met a nice man named Seth Engle. She and Seth decided to get married, and now Seth is my stepfather.

So there are four people in the little house. There are four pets too: Emily Junior, my rat; Bob, Andrew's hermit crab; Midgie, Seth's dog; and Rocky, Seth's cat.

Not long after Mommy married Seth,

Daddy got married again too. That is how Elizabeth Thomas became my stepmother. She and her four children moved into the big house with Daddy. Elizabeth's kids are David Michael, who is seven like me; Kristy, who is thirteen and the best stepsister ever; and Sam and Charlie, who are so old that they are in high school. Then Daddy and Elizabeth adopted Emily Michelle from a faraway country called Vietnam. She is two and a half. I love her so much that I named my pet rat after her.

And then Nannie came to live at the big house too. Nannie is Elizabeth's mother. That makes her my stepgrandmother. (Are you keeping all of this straight? There will be a quiz afterward. Just kidding!) Nannie helps take care of everybody.

There are lots of pets at the big house. They are Shannon, David Michael's big Bernese mountain dog puppy; Pumpkin, a black kitten; Crystal Light the Second, my goldfish; and Goldfishie, Andrew's guess what.

Emily Junior, Bob, Andrew, and I switch houses almost every month. We spend one month at the big house, then one month at the little house. That's why I gave Andrew and me special names. I call us Andrew Two-Two and Karen Two-Two. (I thought up those names after my teacher read a book to our class. It was called *Jacob Two-Two Meets the Hooded Fang*.) I call us those names because we have two of so many things. We have two houses, two mommies, and two daddies. We have two sets of toys and clothes and books. I have two stuffed cats. Goosie lives at the little house. Moosie lives at the big house.

I also have two best friends. Hannie Papadakis lives across the street and one house over from the big house. Nancy Dawes lives next door to the little house. We spend so much time together that we call ourselves the Three Musketeers.

Breakfast at the little house is a lot quieter than at the big house. Everything is quieter there. Especially holidays. At the little

10

house, Christmas is a time to be together and think about how lucky we are. It is calm and beautiful. But at the big house, there are so many people and animals and guests and excitement and presents that Christmas is like a monthlong party.

Both kinds of Christmas are fun. One is not better than the other. But they sure are different. Just like my two houses!

The Karen Chart

After breakfast I went upstairs. I had helped to clear the table. And I had wiped the kitchen table with a dish towel. In a little while I would meet Hannie and Nancy for sledding. (Today was Saturday. If it were a weekday, I would be getting ready to catch the school bus.)

As I went upstairs, I did some thinking. You see, the thing is, most of the time I am as good as any seven-year-old can be. But every once in a while things don't go exactly the way I have planned. I make a mistake, or I make the wrong decision. Then it looks as if I am not totally, one hundred percent good.

Yes, it is true. I will admit it. I am not always perfect. Sometimes, in fact, without really meaning to be, I am naughty. (Some people — and I am not saying who — think I get into trouble *a lot*.) And that could be dangerous in the month of December.

There was no way I wanted to end up on Santa's "naughty" list. Children on the "naughty" list get nothing but coal and straw in their stockings. Now, there was no way for me to tell when Santa might be checking up on me. I had no control over that.

But I did have control over whether I was being naughty or nice most of the time. Which is why I had started my Karen-on-her-best-behavior month. But what if I goofed? What if I was going along, thinking I was being good, when I had actually started to be a tiny bit bad and had not even noticed?

This worried me. I could ask Hannie and Nancy to keep an eye on me and warn me if I started to slip. But Hannie and Nancy could not be around every minute of the day. No one could. So how would I solve this problem?

As I thought this over, my eyes fell on my job chart. Elizabeth had bought it for me to help me remember my family chores. I got a gold star every time I finished one of the jobs on the chart. When I had twenty gold stars, I got to pick what dessert our family would have after dinner. (I usually pick ice-cream sundaes.)

Bing! (That was the sound of an idea hitting my brain.) I could make a Goodness Chart for myself! On it I could mark every time I did something good, or any time I did something less good. The chart would help me keep track of which of Santa's lists I was on — naughty or nice.

14

Brilliant, brilliant, brilliant! I took out a sheet of clean graph paper and made this chart:

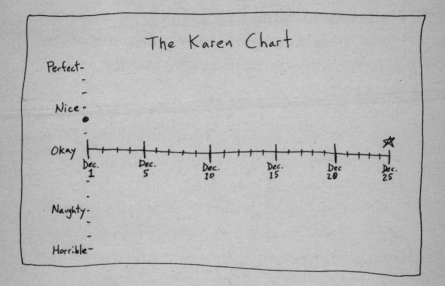

Today was December first. Since I had been so helpful at breakfast, I gave myself a "nice" for the day (so far). I was off to a good start. Now all I had to do was keep it up.

I slipped the Karen Chart into my desk

drawer. What a relief. It was only the first day of the month, and I already had things under control. I walked to the window and peered out. The snow on the ground looked perfect for sledding.

"Here comes the all-new and improved Karen!" I called, running downstairs.

4

Ms. Colman's Announcement

"Eeew! Bobby, that is disgusting!" Pamela Harding wrinkled her nose. "Pick that gum off the floor and throw it away."

Bobby Gianelli laughed. "You pick it up, Gumela!"

A couple of the other boys laughed at what Bobby had called Pamela. I did not laugh, even though Pamela was my best enemy. Did *not* doing something mean count as much as doing something good? I was not sure.

It was Monday morning. Ms. Colman, my wonderful second-grade teacher, would be coming in the door at any second.

"I am not touching your gross gum," said Pamela. "And you had better put it in the trash can where it belongs, or you will be in trouble when Ms. Colman gets here."

"Nyah, nyah!" Bobby jeered. He and the boys cracked up.

Pamela was right, though. Ms. Colman would be mad at Bobby if he left gum on the floor. He would be in trouble. (Have you ever noticed that while gum is in your mouth, it seems delicious? But once it is out of your mouth, all of a sudden, it seems gross? I guess it has something to do with spit.)

Anyway, I wondered if Santa was watching my class at that very moment. Maybe he was, and maybe he was not. Just in case he was, I knew what I had to do — no matter how disgusting.

I took a tissue out of my pocket and picked Bobby's yucky gum off the floor. I

18

tossed the tissue and the gum into the trash can.

"There," I said to Bobby and Pamela. "Now no one will get in trouble." And I have done a good deed, I added silently.

Bobby muttered, "Thanks."

But Pamela looked at me as if she thought I were crazy. "Why did you do that, Karen?" She shook her head. "You are a weirdo."

I was about to call her a name back when I remembered that Santa might be watching. So I did not. I turned and walked away, without saying anything.

I decided to give myself a point for the gum, and half a point for not calling names.

Ms. Colman arrived then, wearing a bright red sweater with a candy cane on it. Terri Barkan took attendance. When she was finished, Ms. Colman stood at the front of the room. "Class, I have a Special Announcement," she said.

Oh, goody! I thought. I love Special Announcements.

"This year Stoneybrook Academy will

present a holiday pageant for parents and friends of the school," Ms. Colman said. "Each class will perform a skit, sing a song, or make some other holiday presentation."

Hands shot up all over the room.

"What are we going to do for our presentation?" half the kids in the class hollered. (I did not. Since I was being good, I remembered not to call out in class. It was amazing.)

"Indoor voices, please," said Ms. Colman. (I love it when someone else is reminded to use an indoor voice.) "We will decide as a class what we will do," Ms. Colman continued. "So, for the next few days, I want each of you to think of ideas for the holiday pageant. Next Monday we will discuss the ideas in class and choose the one that we like the most."

Oh, boy! This was going to be so much fun. I was sure I could come up with a holiday pageant idea that everyone would love. And as star of the show, I would be able to prove to Santa how much I belonged on the nice list. Would we put on a skit? Sing a song? Maybe recite a poem or two? There were so many possibilities!

I raised my arms and pretended to lower a thinking cap onto my head. It was only the third of December, and so far the month had been terrific.

5

Up and Down

For the rest of the week, I was careful to be extra-special good. I am not saying it was easy. But I did it. I hoped that Santa had noticed. But if he had not, I figured, he could always glance at my Karen Chart.

I never forgot to make my bed. I set the table before dinner. I cleared my place after every meal. I gave Shannon her dog food and Pumpkin her cat food. I cleaned out Pumpkin's litter box. (Yuck!) I put away my laundry. I did not leave messes all over the house. I did not leave my schoolbooks on the stairs. I did not even argue with Andrew over who got the last fudgey mallow cookie. (And I wanted it badly.)

On Saturday, I decided to earn extra points by cleaning the bathroom. (David Michael, Andrew, Emily Michelle, and I share one bathroom. Kristy, Sam, and Charlie share the other one. Theirs is always a wreck.)

After I put on some long rubber gloves, I scrubbed, scrubbed, scrubbed the tub. I tried to whistle while I worked, but it still was not too fun. I swept the floor. I put out fresh towels for each of us. I Windexed the mirror. That part was fun.

I had just finished wiping down the counter and polishing the faucet when Emily Michelle came into the bathroom.

"Pay watah!" she said. She picked up her little step stool, the one I used to use, and put it in front of the sink. "Pay watah, Kahwen!"

"No, we are not going to play with water right now, Emily," I said. "I just cleaned this

24

sink, and I do not want it to get messy again."

I picked up the stool and moved it back to the corner of the bathroom. I decided to empty the wastebasket.

"No! Pay!" said Emily Michelle. She got the stool and brought it back to the sink. "Go way!" She glared at me and stuck out her lower lip. Then she stepped up on the stool and leaned forward to turn on the tap. She was going to mess up the whole bathroom!

"Emily Michelle," I said firmly, "I know you do not think you are going to make a mess. But you will, and I am not going to let you."

I picked up Emily from behind and started carrying her out of the bathroom.

Well, I do not know if you have ever carried a two-year-old away from a sink that she thought she was going to play in. But if you have not, let me tell you that the two-year-old will kick and scream.

"Stop!" Emily screamed between sobs.

"Stop! Pay watah! Pay watah! Mommy! Mommmmyyy!"

Elizabeth hurried up the stairs. "What is all this fussing about?"

"Pay watah!" Emily Michelle cried.

"Emily wanted to turn on the water in the sink, and I would not let her," I explained.

Elizabeth picked up Emily and hugged her. Emily snorfled into her shoulder.

"Karen, it is okay if Emily plays in the sink a little," Elizabeth said. "It is just water. It will not hurt anything. And she never makes too big a mess."

"But, but — " I started to say. "I just cleaned up in there."

"That was very nice, Karen," said Elizabeth. "And I appreciate it. Thank you. But Emily *is* allowed to play in the sink."

Emily Michelle peeked out from Elizabeth's shoulder and said, "Meanie-mo!" Then she burst into tears again.

"Okay," said Elizabeth soothingly. "Karen did not intend to be mean." She carried

Emily into the bathroom and set her back on the stool.

".Pay watah!" said Emily Michelle happily.

I wondered if Santa thought I had been mean too. I hoped not. But maybe he had. I sighed. I took away a couple of the day's points.

Then, later that afternoon, I was setting the table, as I did every day. David Michael stormed into the dining room and said, "Drop that spoon, Karen!"

I did. It clattered to the floor. "Why?" I asked.

"I am supposed to set the table," said David Michael. "So far I have not been able to do it even once this week. If you do not stop stealing my chores, I am not going to get my allowance."

Ohhhh. I had forgotten that David Michael would not get his allowance unless he did all his chores himself.

I handed him the silverware (he picked up the spoon himself) and said, "Here. You

28

may do it. I was not trying to steal your chore."

"Thanks," David Michael muttered as he laid down a fork.

Gosh. Two of my good deeds had backfired. That night, I looked at my Karen Chart. I had not meant to be naughty — it had just turned out that way. I was still doing really well, according to the chart.

But I had had some close calls.

Minus, Minus, Minus

"Would you like me to do that for you?" I asked Sam.

Sam looked up. He was polishing the blade of his ice-hockey skate. "No thank you, Karen. It was nice of you to ask, though."

I know it was, I said to myself. Santa, are you watching?

I went into the kitchen, where Daddy was slicing some radishes for a salad.

"Can I help you with that?" I asked.

"I had better do it," said Daddy. "This knife is pretty sharp. Thanks for asking."

"Elizabeth? Do you need me to do anything?" She was bustling around, getting out bowls and spices.

"No thanks, Karen," said Elizabeth. "It will be easier for me to make this meat loaf myself."

Hmph. There had to be somebody who needed my help. How was I going to show Santa how good I was if no one ever let me do a good deed?

Just then Elizabeth turned to reach for the salt and practically crashed right into me.

"Karen, your father and I are working in the kitchen," said Elizabeth. "If you do not have a reason to be in here . . ."

"Okay, okay," I said. "I will get out of your way." I slumped out of the kitchen and into the living room.

"Nannie?" I asked. "Anything I can do to help?"

Nannie put down the magazine she had

been reading. "Trying to make yourself use-ful, are you, Karen?" she asked.

I nodded.

"Okay, tell you what. We need to clean the house. This weekend we will put up our Christmas decorations, and I want the house looking its best. I will vacuum the dining room while you dust the living room. How does that sound?"

"Great," I said, giving Nannie a big smile. I was glad that someone was willing to let me do something nice!

I got a feather duster, a dust rag, and a can of furniture polish out of the utility closet. I helped Nannie lug the vacuum into the dining room.

Nannie clicked on the vacuum, which started to roar. I walked back into the living room and began dusting.

I kind of like dusting. It is not as much fun as raking leaves or shoveling snow, but it is definitely better than cleaning the bath-tub. I like the lemony, woody smell of furni-ture polish.

I wiped the two end tables and the coffee table with the dust rag. I polished the bases of all the lamps in the room. I feather-dusted the lamp shades. I straightened the throw pillows and cushions on the sofa and easy chairs.

I found three nickels, two pennies, and a dime underneath the cushions. I decided to give them to charity, even before I remembered about Santa Claus watching me. Score another point for Karen!

I gazed around the living room. It looked spotless. No dust on any surfaces.

Then I realized there was a surface I could not see — the top of the mantel over the fireplace. (The big house has several gigundo old marble mantelpieces.) This mantel was where we hung our stockings with care. When Santa was filling stockings, he would be sure to notice if the mantel was dirty. I did not want him to think the Brewer-Thomases were slobs.

I reached up on tiptoe and started to sweep back and forth across the top of the mantel with the feather duster. I could not really see what I was doing, but I hoped I was getting most of the dust.

Suddenly I heard — *crash!*

Uh-oh. Glass and water had showered down on the hearth, and several roses were scattered on the floor.

I had broken a glass vase.

And then I had a terrible thought. I remembered Nannie talking about an antique crystal vase that she had inherited from her grandmother. I knew it was special and could not be replaced.

I almost burst into tears. I had smashed Nannie's antique crystal vase! I did not know what to do. The vacuum was still roaring in the dining room. I did not think anyone had heard the crash when the vase fell.

What to do, what to do? I was not thinking straight. I needed time to figure out how to tell Nannie that I had destroyed her grandmother's vase.

I dashed to the garage, where the newspa-

34

pers were waiting to be recycled. I grabbed a couple of sections. I raced back to the living room and carefully (very carefully, so I did not cut myself on broken glass) scooped the glass and roses onto a section of newspaper. I blotted up the water with my dust cloth.

Then I carefully carried the whole mess upstairs to my room. When I got there, I did not know what to do with it. So I shoved it under my bed.

I would deal with it later.

7

A Reindeer!

Later that night I took out my Karen Chart. I thought of all the good things I had done that day:

I had helped Nannie clean the house.

I had said "please," "thank you," and "you're welcome" every time I should have.

I had picked up Emily Michelle and comforted her when she had fallen down.

I had helped Andrew clean the playroom even though I had not made the mess in there.

Then I listed the bad things I had done:

I had broken Nannie's vase and hidden the evidence.

On the bright side, my good things outnumbered my bad things. But all my good things were little, and my one bad thing was a whopper.

My chart now looked like this:

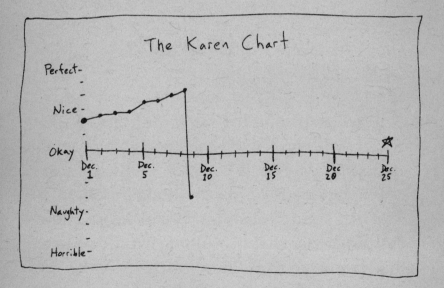

How could I make up for what I had done? I could not fix the vase — it was in a million pieces. And I could not buy Nannie a vase to replace it.

Maybe I could buy her a vase that would be almost as nice. But that would cost more money than I had, I was sure. Vases were expensive, weren't they? And if I spent all my money on a new vase, how would I buy Christmas gifts for everyone else? I was stuck.

I looked at my chart one last time, then put it back in my desk drawer. I climbed into bed and turned out the light. But I could not stop thinking about my chart. There were a lot of naughty points on it now. So where did I stand with Santa?

I lay awake in bed, tossing and turning.

What if no one found out about the broken vase until after Christmas? What if Santa did not find out either? Well, I knew that was impossible. Nannie would notice that her vase was missing. And Santa always knows when you have been good or bad. He knows when you are sleeping. He even knows when you are awake way past your bedtime, like I was at that moment.

I started to wonder whether I was going

to get any Christmas presents at all. Santa knew I had been a lot more naughty than nice. I thought so much that I gave myself a stomachache. I sat up and pushed aside the curtain to my window. I loved seeing the moonlight on the snow outside.

There was a line of trees at the back of the big-house yard. They looked beautiful in the moonlight with the snow on their branches. Then I frowned and squinted. I saw a big, dark shape moving through the trees. Was it a person? Somebody's dog?

No . . . it was much too big to be a dog. It was even too big to be a person. My breath froze in my throat. Was it a bear?

Then the whatever-it-was stepped out from under the trees and into the moonlight. I could see it clearly. It was tall and a little shaggy, and it had antlers.

I could not believe my eyes. It was a reindeer. A real, live reindeer.

"Oh, my goodness!" I whispered to myself. A reindeer in my own backyard! Reindeer do not live in Connecticut. Reindeer live way up north, like at the . . . North Pole!

I gasped. My brain started whirring. Then I realized that this must be one of Santa's reindeer.

I sat perfectly still, staring at it. I felt that if I blinked, the reindeer would disappear. Finally I let out a breath — and just like that, the reindeer spun around and bolted into the woods.

A huge smile came over my face, and I was filled with a warm, happy feeling. I had seen one of Santa's reindeer! It was a Christmas miracle.

Then I thought of something: What was one of Santa's reindeer doing in Stoneybrook?

Rudolph

"We could have a Kwanzaa celebration," said Sara Ford.

It was Monday, and the kids in Ms. Colman's class were talking about our holiday pageant. Today was the day we would vote for the best idea.

"We could teach the Seven Principles of Kwanzaa," Sara continued. "There are lots of great crafts and activities we could do."

"That sounds like fun," said Ian Johnson.

"Well, I was thinking I could dress up like High-style Brittany," said Pamela. "She is my new fashion doll. The other girls could dress up like Sandy, Brittany's personal assistant."

I rolled my eyes but did not say anything. I was still trying to be good.

"Yeah? And what would the boys do?" Hank Reubens asked Pamela. "Sit around and watch?"

"Exactly," said Pamela. "You could watch, as long as you did not get in the way."

"My idea is to do a Toy Wars skit," said Bobby. "We will dress up like Power Morphers and pretend the evil Dr. Maligno has taken over the North Pole, trapped all the elves, and turned Santa's workshop into an Ice Fortress. We could have a huge battle, with snow cannons and exploding ice and — "

Bobby went on and on about his Toy Wars skit. Then Ricky Torres talked about his idea for a mini Winter Olympics, with a bobsled run down the center aisle of the school auditorium. Natalie Springer's idea was to act out the manger scene in which the Three Wise Men come to see the baby Jesus.

I was not paying much attention to what everyone was saying. I was too busy thinking about the vase I had broken the day before — and about the reindeer I had seen.

I heard Nancy say, "My idea is to do something in honor of Hanukkah. I was thinking that nine of us could dress up like the candles on a menorah."

I thought that was a great idea. But then my mind wandered some more.

Would Nannie forgive me? Would Santa forgive me? Could I manage to be good for the rest of December? And why was one of Santa's reindeer in my backyard?

I had a terrible thought then. But suddenly everything made sense. Santa couldn't possibly watch me all the time, checking whether I was naughty or nice. He had too many other kids to keep track of. But what if some of his reindeer helped him watch? What if this reindeer was . . . a spy? If that was true, it knew all about the terrible thing I had done. It had probably heard the vase crash, even over the roar of the vacuum cleaner in the next room. (Animals have very good hearing, you know.)

And if the reindeer knew about it, chances were it would tell Santa. Unless I fixed things, I would get straw and coal for Christmas.

I wondered which reindeer I had seen. Dasher? Donner? Blitzen? Or could it have been . . . oh, my goodness!

"Rudolph!" I blurted out. I practically shouted it, forgetting to use my indoor voice.

Everyone turned toward me. Nancy, who had been describing how the menorah candles would dance in a chorus line, fell silent.

"Rudolph?" repeated Ricky Torres. "Hey, that is a great idea, Karen. We could sing 'Rudolph the Red-Nosed Reindeer' and act it out."

"Yes, that would be so much fun!" said Addie Sidney.

"What a brilliant idea!" "Cool!" "I want to be Comet!"

Everyone started talking about what a

great idea I had come up with. Everyone, that is, except Nancy. Nancy looked hurt.

"It was an accident," I said quickly to Nancy. "I was thinking out loud. I did not mean to suggest 'Rudolph the Red-Nosed Reindeer.' I would rather be a Hanukkah candle! Honestly!"

Nancy said, "That is okay, Karen." But her voice told me it was not okay.

I had done one more bad thing without meaning to. And a reindeer spy had probably delivered its report on me by now. Santa would not be happy. I probably would not get another Christmas gift until I was ten years old!

9

The Christmas Spirit

Although on Monday I felt very unhappy, my spirits had lifted a bit by Tuesday. As I said, I am a naturally cheerful person. I am also very determined. On Monday evening I gave myself a little pep talk. I pointed out how good I had been for almost two whole weeks. I pointed out that I still had almost two weeks in which to be extra good. And I figured that Santa could not rely too much on his reindeer's report. After all, he was the one with the list that he checked twice. He would be watching me again before Christmas. I was sure of it. And I was going to be ready. I was going to be better than ever.

So on Tuesday I helped Nannie fix everyone's school lunches. I tied Andrew's shoes for him. I let Emily Michelle watch her favorite TV show after I got home from school, even though I was trying to do my homework. I would not let a little trouble get me down. No way!

Thank heavens, no disasters happened on Tuesday or Wednesday. When I got home from school on Wednesday afternoon, I found Nannie in the mudroom, surrounded by boxes of lights and outdoor decorations. Today we were going to decorate the outside of the house for Christmas. There is nothing that gives me Christmas spirit more than hanging up mistletoe and holly.

Nannie placed holly boughs on the mailbox. David Michael put the big pinecone wreath on the front door. And Andrew and I hung red ribbons everywhere. Later, Sam, Charlie, and Daddy hung twinkling Christmas lights on our house. Elizabeth and Kristy draped more lights on our trees and bushes. Everything looked so, so Christmassy! I felt my spirits soar.

Before it was time to go inside for supper, I checked our backyard for reindeer hoofprints. Maybe I would be able to find out what the reindeer was doing here. Maybe I could catch it trying to spy on me! Or maybe it was in trouble and needed my help.

Later I tried to read a book, but I could not concentrate on it. I kept wondering about Santa's reindeer. I had decided that it probably was not Rudolph, since I had not seen a glowing red nose. And I had begun to think I was wrong about the reindeer being a spy. Spying was just too un-Santaish. Sure, the song says that Santa sees you when you are sleeping. But who is ever bad in their sleep? Santa checks in on you when you are sleeping to make sure you are okay — not having a nightmare or coming untucked.

So if the reindeer was not a spy, what was it doing in my backyard? Was *it* okay? Did it miss Santa and want to go home? Was it hungry? I decided to look for him again. Maybe I could lure him with some food.

What did reindeer eat, anyway? Vegetables, I supposed.

I went to the refrigerator and took a bag of baby carrots out of the crisper drawer. Then I ran to where I had seen the reindeer. (I took a bag of recycling with me to disguise what I was doing. I did not want anybody with me right away. One person was bad enough. But two people would definitely scare the reindeer.

It was pretty dark outside, but snow made everything look brighter. Carefully I wandered among the trees at the back of our yard, peering at the ground. I did not see a single thing. More snow had fallen last night, but you'd think a huge reindeer would leave pretty deep prints. Still, I could not find a trace of one.

I waited for what seemed like hours. Then

finally I saw a large dark shape. There it was! Santa's reindeer. I could barely make out its shape but it was definitely there.

But I wanted someone else to see the magical reindeer. I wanted to share it with someone.

"Come quick!" I hollered. "Come see this! Quickly! Come here, everybody!"

I watched the reindeer nibble at the ground. I could not believe it. I was feeding one of Santa's reindeer.

For a few seconds nobody opened my door. Then I heard the latch, and turned to see Charlie in the doorway.

"What is all the fuss?" he asked.

"Come see, Charlie!" I said. "Quick, before the reindeer disappears!"

"Huh?" Charlie said.

"A reindeer! In the backyard. It is one of Santa's! Look!" I turned back to the window and peered out.

I gasped. The reindeer was gone.

Charlie was looking over my shoulder. "I do not see anything," he said. "Except the

backyard. Are you sure you saw a deer, Karen? That is pretty exciting."

"I am sure I saw a deer," I said firmly. "And not just any deer — a reindeer. And not just any reindeer — one of Santa's reindeer."

Charlie looked at me. "Well, you know, deer are pretty common in the woods around here, and sometimes they even come into town. But not reindeer."

"It was a reindeer," I said firmly. I folded my arms across my chest.

Charlie paused for a second. Then he smiled and said, "Okay, it was a reindeer. I believe you. Anything is possible. Now, lie down and try to get some sleep. It is way past your bedtime."

"Okay, Charlie," I said.

Charlie's Dumb Ornament

After school the next day, we decorated the inside of the big house for Christmas. If there is one thing I love more than decorating the outside of a house, it is decorating the inside.

Nannie hung garlands of fir branches along the staircase banister. Kristy twined red velvet ribbon around it. I had a box of little holly sprigs, and I could put them wherever I wanted. Holly is kind of prickly, but it is very pretty.

Sam hung a long garland over the front

door, and Charlie wove tiny lights through it. We put a huge bowl of red apples on the dining room table and tied a bow around the bowl.

Finally, Elizabeth set up the crèche (that is the Christmas manger scene) on the mantelpiece.

I was so, so nervous that Elizabeth would notice that the vase was missing from the mantel. But she did not. And when Nannie looked at the crèche, I was even more nervous. But Nannie did not notice that her vase was missing.

Whew!

Still, worrying about getting caught had brought back all my worries about being naughty. I was determined to be nice for the rest of the month but there was no undoing what I had already done. It is hard to have fun when you are knotted up inside.

That evening Daddy brought a Christmas tree home and set it up.

And now came my most favorite Christmas-decorating time of all: trimming the tree. And Daddy had brought home the biggest, most beautiful tree ever. It was full and round and perfectly tree-shaped, and it had soft blue-green needles that smelled delicious. It was so tall that it almost scraped the ceiling.

Kristy, David Michael, Andrew, and I carefully placed the red and green glass balls and porcelain angels and glass stars and all the other breakable ornaments on the tree. While we were doing that, Emily Michelle put the wooden and cloth ornaments on the lower branches. (Sam and Charlie were at a basketball game, so they were missing all the tree-trimming fun.)

Nannie popped popcorn and Elizabeth heated up some cider with cinnamon sticks in it. Daddy put on some Christmas music. It was so wonderfully Christmassy. Once again I tried to put the vase out of my mind.

I loved looking at all the ornaments. My favorite is a green glass angel blowing a red glass trumpet. It is gigundoly pretty.

I carefully unwrapped the angel from the

tissue paper that had kept it safe in its box in the attic. Then I noticed a bit of orange under the tissue paper.

Orange? I said to myself. That is not a Christmas color.

I unwrapped the orange ornament. Oh, yes. I recognized it. It was Charlie's special New York Knicks (that is a basketball team) ornament, which he has had since he was nine, many years ago. The Knicks' colors are orange and blue.

Now, do not get me wrong. Orange and blue are nice colors. I like orange and blue. It is just that they are not Christmas colors. Christmas colors are red and green. Orange and blue are totally un-Christmassy. They are not even New Year's Evey. (I am not sure what New Year's Eve colors are, but I am sure they are not orange and blue.)

There is nothing very Christmassy about basketball either. But every year, Charlie hangs his un-Christmassy orange-and-blue basketball ornament in the middle of the tree, where everyone can see it.

Well, this was the most beautiful, perfect tree ever, and I was not going to let Charlie's ornament spoil it.

Quickly I stuffed the ornament into my pocket and said, "Um, excuse me, I have to go upstairs for a minute."

I ran upstairs and shoved Charlie's ornament under my bed, next to the newspaper with the broken shards of vase folded inside. Then I tried to forget about it. Just like the vase.

It Must Be Magic

Before climbing into bed that night, I pulled back my curtain. I felt terrible. (Sometimes when you feel terrible, it helps to look out a window.) I knew hiding Charlie's ornament had been bad. It was Christmastime, I was trying my hardest, and I was still doing bad things.

I took one last look at the twinkling lights Daddy had strung everywhere. They were shining on the snow.

Suddenly, through the window, what

should I see but — the reindeer again. This was the second night in a row!

I ran downstairs and found Charlie in the kitchen. He was fixing himself a snack — a giant glass of milk and a sandwich about the size of a brick.

"Charlie!" I said breathlessly.

"Karen!" he said, imitating me. "What is up?"

"The reindeer is in the backyard and I forgot to feed him and he might be hungry but if I go out there now he might be scared and run away and I do not know what to do," I said in a rush.

"Whoa, slow down," said Charlie. "The reindeer is in the backyard, and what is the problem?"

I explained again, slightly more slowly this time. Then I dragged Charlie to the kitchen window.

Just as we reached the window, I saw a flash of motion in the backyard. And then the reindeer was gone.

"Did you see that?" I practically screamed.

"Mwahf?" said Charlie, his mouth full of salami and tomato and lettuce and bread.

"What?" I said.

He swallowed. "I said, What? Did I see what?"

"The reindeer! He was right there! You could not have missed him!"

Charlie shook his head and took another bite. "Norry, Yarum." He swallowed. "Sorry, Karen. I did not see him." He patted my head. "But I believe you did. Honestly. So let's throw some food out there for him. It is a terrible thing to be hungry." He took another huge bite of sandwich and swallowed.

How could the reindeer disappear like that? I wondered. Did it have some magical powers? Well, I mean, of course it did. It was Santa's special flying reindeer.

"There is some celery in the fridge that is looking limp," Charlie said. "It will be just right for the reindeer. You go back to bed. I will put out the celery, okay?"

I nodded. "Okay." I started to leave, then paused in the doorway. "Thanks, Charlie. You are the best."

Charlie smiled. "No problem."

I went back to my room. I was still worried about whether my reindeer would find his way back to the North Pole. But at least I knew he would not go hungry tonight. I could worry about my bad behavior instead. Then suddenly I had a thought. Maybe Santa would forgive me if I took extra-good care of his reindeer.

Yes, that was it. I would spend the rest of the Christmas season helping my reindeer.

12

Elf #4

The next morning I got up early and hung Charlie's ornament on the tree. I stood back and looked at it. Actually, it was not so bad. It sort of blended with all the other colors on the tree. I was glad that I had put it back.

At school Ms. Colman announced that we would pull names out of a hat to choose the parts in our "Rudolph the Red-Nosed Reindeer" show. The parts for the show were:

Santa Claus

Mrs. Claus

Eight reindeer (Prancer, Dancer, Donner, Blitzen, Comet, Cupid, Dasher, Vixen)

Rudolph

Elves

As Ms. Colman passed the hat around, I wished really, really hard that I would pull the name Rudolph from the hat. Rudolph is the star of the show, and I knew I could be the star. I have been in many plays before. Plus, this play had been my idea, even though it had been by accident. I could just see myself wearing a reindeer costume. It would help me show Santa how much good will and Christmas spirit I had. It was true that I had had some setbacks lately in the goodness department. Maybe I would get extra points if I had more Christmas spirit than anyone.

While I waited for the hat, I thought about the real reindeer — Santa's lost reindeer. I would feed it and take care of it until it found its way back to the North Pole. It would be up to me, and me alone, to save Christmas — just like Rudolph did.

I hoped Santa would see the connection between Rudolph and me, the Christmas savers. And that he would understand that, even though I had made a few mistakes, I was not all bad and deserved maybe a present or two.

The hat went around the room. Addie Sidney pulled Santa Claus out of it. Everyone cheered. Her wheelchair would make a perfect sleigh.

Nancy picked Comet. She smiled a big smile. She would make a good reindeer.

As Pamela put her hand in the hat, she said, "Come on, Rudolph!"

I frowned, and said silently to myself, "Come on, elf!"

Pamela read her paper, and her face fell. "Elf Number Three," she said indignantly.

I tried not to feel happy. That would be mean.

Prancer, Vixen, and Donner were chosen next.

When the hat finally reached me, Rudolph still had not been chosen. I crossed my fingers and hoped hard.

I reached in and pulled out a slip of paper. I unfolded it. It said:

ELF #4

Elf Number Four? I frowned. How could that be? If this were some other play, I would love being an elf. Elves are cute. But I was supposed to be Rudolph. And if I could not be Rudolph, I wanted at least to be a reindeer, like Prancer or Dancer. (I am very good at prancing and dancing.)

But Elf Number Four? I might as well play a piece of scenery, for all the attention I would get.

Worst of all, I would have to stand next to Pamela — Elf Number Three — during the show.

As I sat stewing, the hat went around the

classroom. I heard someone squeal with delight. I turned around: It was Hannie.

"I got Rudolph!" she said.

My very own best friend would be playing the part I had wanted so much. Did Hannie have her very own reindeer in her own backyard? No. Had Hannie thought of this play in the first place? No. Was Hannie going to save Santa's reindeer, just like Santa's reindeer had saved Christmas? No. And yet she was going to be the star of the show. Does that sound fair? No.

But I had to be nice. (You know why.)

"Congratulations, Hannie," I said to her at recess that day. "I am sure you will make a wonderful Rudolph."

"Thanks, Karen," said Hannie. "And I am sure you will make a wonderful elf."

13

At Bellair's

On Wednesday Nannie took David Michael, Andrew, and me shopping at Bellair's, the big department store in downtown Stoneybrook. I love Bellair's, especially the floor with all the mattresses. It is fun to try them out.

Like almost everything else, Bellair's is especially wonderful at Christmastime. The store is decorated with red ribbons and holly, and Christmas carols play constantly. I can never get enough carols at Christmas.

I wanted to give presents to so many people that I could not possibly buy gifts for all of them. Most of the people on my list would get homemade things. For instance, I was planning on making fancy paper angels, decorated with glitter and Day-Glo markers, for Hannie and Nancy. I was sure they would love them. (Nancy celebrates Hanukkah. I was going to give her her angel on the first day of Hanukkah.)

But I did have enough money to buy a few nice gifts. I was thinking about new mittens for Andrew, and an action figure for David Michael. Elizabeth likes jewelry, so a light-up Santa Claus pin would be perfect for her.

"Now, I want everyone to stick together," said Nannie as we entered the store. I groaned. How could I buy things for David Michael and Andrew without their knowing it? I whispered this to Nannie. Luckily, David Michael was most interested in playing the video games set up in the electronic-toy section, and Nannie managed

71

to distract Andrew while I chose a pair of snowflake mittens for him. So I bought my gifts.

But I felt guilty spending my Christmas money on gifts when I did not know how I was going to replace the vase I had broken. But I figured that, even if I had enough money to buy a new crystal vase (and I did not), it would never be as special as the one I had broken. Plus, I would not have any money left over for presents. And Santa would want me to be generous to my friends and family.

So I spent the money on gifts and tried not to think about the vase.

After we finished shopping, Nannie said, "And now, how about a special treat?"

"Yea!" I said. "Ice cream!"

Nannie laughed. "No, not ice cream. I was thinking of something even better. We can go to see Santa Claus."

Both Andrew and I shouted "Yea!"

David Michael started to shout "Yea" too.

Then he stopped. He said, "I am too old to sit on Santa's lap. It is for babies."

"It is not for babies," I said. "I am not a baby, and I am not too old to sit on Santa's lap. I will not be too old even when I am a hundred. I will always love Santa." So there, I added silently.

David Michael shrugged. "You go on, then. I will stay with Nannie."

Andrew and I got in line, and before I knew it, I was climbing up onto Santa's lap.

Now, I know that the Bellair's Santa is not the real, genuine Santa who lives at the North Pole. After all, every department store has a Santa, and you see Santas on lots of street corners. Awhile ago, I figured out that the Bellair's Santa, and all those other Santas, are like the elves. They are the real Santa's helpers. They do good deeds and listen to children. They make sure that everything is ready for the big night. They help Christmas run smoothly.

"Hello, little girl," Santa said, chuckling a couple of ho-ho-hos. "What is your name?"

"Karen Brewer," I said. I put my hand on his shoulder. "Do not worry. I am taking care of your reindeer."

"Reindeer?" said Santa. "Ho, ho, ho. What reindeer?"

"The reindeer that is lost," I said. "It has been coming around my backyard. I am feeding it — and saving Christmas." I winked at him. "You can tell me — which is it? Comet? Cupid? I bet it is Cupid."

Santa looked confused, as if he did not know what I was talking about. "Yes, sure. Cupid. Now, ho, ho, ho, what did you want for Christmas, little girl?"

I could tell that Santa did not know whether it was Cupid or not. The real Santa, up at the North Pole, needed to let his helpers know what was going on. The Bellair's Santa was totally clueless.

"I just want to save Christmas," I said modestly. Then I patted him on the shoulder and said, "Put in a good word for me with the real Santa, okay?"

I hopped off his lap. A successful visit with Santa Claus, if I do say so myself. Even if Santa did seem a little confused.

14

Can Hannie Fly?

On Friday we rehearsed our "Rudolph the Red-Nosed Reindeer" show.

Ms. Colman had come up with some simple steps for the reindeer to perform while they were singing. They would paw at the ground with their hooves, then take two little prancing steps forward. It did look very reindeerish. Once again, I wished that I could have been a reindeer — any reindeer.

As an elf, I was just supposed to stand in the background with my hands clasped behind my back and sing.

It was difficult for me to stay in the background like a good Elf Number Four. So I kept edging forward, taking little steps when the reindeer did. That is how it is when you want to be the star.

Also, I was sure Santa would give me some kind of signal that he knew I was trying to save Christmas. And the best, clearest signal he could send would be to let me be Rudolph, the saver of Christmas (and star of the show). I knew Hannie was *supposed* to play Rudolph. But somehow Santa would come through with that sign. I just knew it.

Pamela, who was supposed to stand next to me in the back, kept pushing forward. It was very annoying. Whenever she would move in front of me a little, *I* would step around *her*. Then she would step in front of me again. I could not believe her nerve!

Finally Pamela hissed, "Get back!" and threw her arm in front of me. She tried to push me back toward the other elves. I grabbed Pamela's arm and yanked her in back of me. Then I began singing extra loudly.

Ms. Colman stepped forward and clapped her hands to stop the music. She said, "Karen, Pamela, if you cannot stop disrupting the rehearsal, I will have to ask you both to take a seat."

I was gigundoly embarrassed. I think Pamela was too, though she whispered, "Yeah, Karen, stop it!"

Since it was December, I did not say anything. I shuffled backward next to my fellow elf Ricky Torres, and tried to stay there.

The climax of the show came when Hannie-as-Rudolph guided Santa's sleigh through the fog. Ms. Colman said that for the actual performance we would borrow a fog machine. Underneath her Rudolph costume, Hannie would wear a harness attached to a wire. The wire would lift Hannie up off the stage, so she could fly like a real flying reindeer. Then she would pull Addie and her wheelchair across the stage, below her.

I was so, so envious. How I wanted to fly through the air, above the crowd, all eyes on me! It would be so much fun, like being in a real Broadway play in New York.

"Fly?" Hannie said when Ms. Colman told her about the wire. She looked a little scared.

"You will be lifted up only a few feet off the ground," Ms. Colman said. "It is completely safe."

With the help of Mr. Wickersham, another teacher, Ms. Colman strapped Hannie into the harness. It looked like the kind of halter a small dog would use, with straps around Hannie's chest and waist, joined by other straps so she would be comfortable. It looked very sturdy. I was practically green with envy as I sang about Rudolph's nose being so bright. Mr. Wickersham pulled on a cable backstage, and Hannie was lifted gently into the air.

"Aieee!" Hannie shrieked. She kicked her legs and flailed her arms, not looking a thing like a reindeer. "Put me down!"

Ms. Colman grabbed Hannie. Mr. Wickersham let down the cable, and Ms. Colman
lowered Hannie safely to the stage floor.
"Goodness, are you all right, Hannie?" she
asked.

Hannie nodded. "Yes, I am okay. I was
just a little startled. That is all."

She looked very nervous and unsure, I
thought.

"Do you think you will be able to fly on
the night of the performance?" asked Ms.
Colman.

Hannie hesitated, then nodded. "I can do
it."

Inside, my heart was breaking. Sure, Hannie could do it. But would she do it as well
as I could, with all my Christmas spirit
and stage experience? No. That was the sad
truth.

15

The Chart of Doom

That weekend I took out the Karen Chart to see how I was doing on the naughty/nice scale.

I bit my lip as I looked at it. I was not doing very well.

At first I had gone up, up, up. Then I had begun to drop way down. I had gone up a little, then down. Up a little more, then waaayyy down. Now I was solidly in the naughty zone. If Santa checked my name on his list now, I would get nothing in my stocking but coal and straw. I had to raise

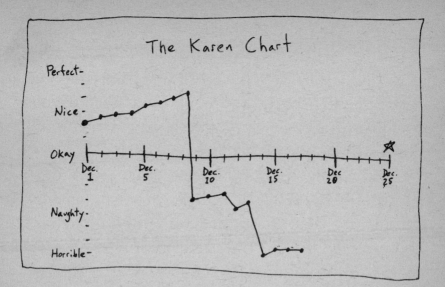

The Karen Chart

Perfect-

Nice-

Okay

Dec. 1   Dec. 5   Dec. 10   Dec. 15   Dec. 20   Dec. 25

Naughty-

Horrible-

my score — and fast. There were only a few days left before Christmas.

I decided to go on a do-or-die niceness campaign. I would be super helpful and super good, even if it killed me.

The first thing I did was see if anything needed cleaning in the kitchen. (There are so many people in the big house that the kitchen is almost always cluttered.) When I looked around, though, I was disappointed to see no crumbs on the table, no dishes in the sink, no unwiped spills on the counter.

83

I opened the dishwasher. Aha! I would put the dishes away.

They did not seem all that clean (maybe we needed to get a new dishwasher), especially the silverware. But I put everything back in its place.

Whistling happily, I went into the living room, to see what I could do there. I was not going to dust, though. I remembered what happened the last time I did that.

A few minutes later, as I was straightening magazines in the magazine rack, I heard Elizabeth exclaim, "Oh, yuck! Who took the dirty dishes out of the dishwasher and put them in the cupboard?"

Uh-oh. No wonder they seemed dirty. I could feel myself piling up more naughty points. Why did these things keep happening to me? Quickly I gathered up some old magazines and scurried out of the living room.

I dropped the magazines into my wagon and walked down the street to the recycling center. I slipped them through the slot, into the big metal bin that holds recyclable paper. Surely this would count as nice. After all, recycling is good for the entire planet.

When I returned to the big house, Daddy was in the living room scratching his head. "Has anyone seen my new issue of *Forbes* magazine?" he asked. "And I seem to be missing my new *Sports Illustrated* and *Newsweek* too."

Oh, my gosh! What had I done now? I was turning into a walking disaster. I should have a CAUTION sign attached to me! I dashed upstairs before Daddy could see me blushing. But the awfulness did not stop there.

On Sunday evening I very responsibly did a load of laundry. I measured the soap carefully and made sure there was nothing delicate in the batch. But I forgot to take out one red shirt. I turned everyone's under-wear pink! Elizabeth, Kristy, Emily Michelle, and I did not mind. Some of our underwear is pink anyway. But Sam, Charlie, David Michael, Andrew, and Daddy were not very thrilled.

"Um, I think it's pretty," I said lamely as Sam glared at me.

"There is no way I'm wearing this in the locker room!" he complained, and threw his pink shorts back into the hamper. I felt miserable.

That evening I took a look at my revised chart. I had racked up so many naughty points that I had to tape a new piece of graph paper to the bottom of the old one.

I had been so naughty that I probably would not be getting anything from Santa until I was thirty. The worst thing was, I had been sliding downhill even while I was trying extra hard to be nice. That afternoon I had tossed some radishes in the yard for the reindeer. The way things were going, I would not be surprised to find out that radishes are poisonous to reindeer. Santa would never give me anything again!

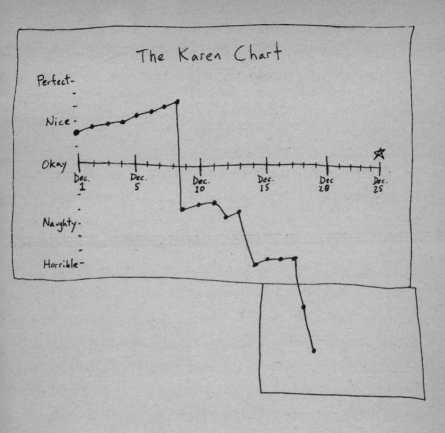

The Karen Chart

Rudolph the Runny-Nosed Reindeer

On Tuesday night I was sitting in my room wrapping presents. I am a very good wrapper. My bows are especially bouncy. Sadly I taped David Michael's package closed. How nice that other people would be getting gifts, I thought. At least my family and friends would enjoy Christmas, even if I myself would not. But I was not going to give up. I would try to be extra nice until the bitter end. In my mind I pictured myself opening my stocking. "Oh, a lovely piece of coal!" I saw myself saying. "And some straw! It seems very fresh! Thank you, Santa!"

I almost burst into tears just thinking about it.

The next day was the last day of school before winter break. Our school's holiday show would be held in the evening. I still wished I could have been Rudolph, or at least one of the other reindeer. A back-of-the-stage elf was just not much fun. I would have been a fabulous Rudolph, compared to —

But I was trying not to think bad thoughts about anyone else in the show. Super nice, remember?

I let out a long, deep sigh and curled the ends of a ribbon.

The phone rang, and I heard Elizabeth call, "Karen! The phone is for you."

I leaped up and ran down the hall to the phone.

"Hello?" I said.

"Hello, Kared," said someone.

"Hannie? Is that you?" I asked.

"Yes. Kared, I have a cold."

"You have a cold?" I repeated.

"Yes. With a stuffed-up dose," said Hannie. "I do dot doe if I will be able to go od stage toborrow dight."

"Oh, no! That is terrible."

"Yes," said Hannie. "It is a shabe. But I was thickig. Baybe you should play Rudolph. 'Rudolph the Red-Dose Reiddeer' was your idea id the first place."

My heart leaped. I could not believe it! "Oh, boy! Are you sure?" I cried. "I would love to! I know the part by heart!" Then I remembered that Hannie was not feeling well. And she was probably very disappointed that she would not be able to be in the show. "I mean, do not worry. I will fill in for you. The show must go on. I am so sorry that you will not be in it, though."

"Oh, I will be id it," said Hannie. "I ab dot that sick. I just thick a sballer role would be better. We could trade. You be Rudolph, ad I will be Elf Nubber Four. Okay?"

A shiver went down my spine. This was

the very sign from Santa that I had been waiting for! Maybe he would send another one during the show.

"Okay!" I said. "That would be fine."

"Great," said Hannie. "By bother said she would call Bs. Colbad and let her doe about the chage."

"I will tell my daddy too," I said. "See you tomorrow, Hannie. I hope you feel better."

"I will be fide. Just dot fide enough to fly arond, that is all."

I hung up the phone and raced to tell Daddy and everyone else about being Rudolph. They seemed happy for me.

That night, before I went to bed, I put on my snow boots and heavy coat and brought some food out to my reindeer. I left a head of cabbage, some oatmeal, and two corn muffins for it. "Enjoy!" I called softly into the darkness.

Then I went upstairs, snuggled under my covers, and went to sleep happy for the first time in weeks.

17

Reindeer Games

"Is everyone ready?" Ms. Colman asked. "We will go on in about five minutes."

I nodded, looking at myself in the mirror. I looked great — very reindeerish. All of us reindeers were wearing zip-up reindeer suits. We looked like a herd of special, magical reindeer all right. But there were two differences between my reindeer friends and me: One, underneath my costume I was wearing my flying harness. Two, everyone else had black noses. My nose was bright, shiny red. I felt very special.

After all, I was sure this was Santa's sign I was doing something right. He must have seen me on my good days and rewarded me with the part of Rudolph. I still wondered if he would send me another sign during the show. Maybe something magical would happen.

"You look great, Karen!" said Hannie. She was dressed in a red and green elf costume.

"Thank you," I said. "How are you feeling?"

"Huh?" she asked, looking confused. "Oh! Yes, well, I feel much better today," she said quickly. "I feel almost fine. Not fine enough to be Rudolph. But fine enough for an elf."

"Oh, good. Thank you for asking me to be Rudolph. It means more to me than you know." I gave her a hug.

"That is okay," she said. "I am glad you could do it."

The first act in our holiday show was the kindergartners. They sang "Frosty the

Snowman." After them, the first-graders sang "The Little Drummer Boy." They were pretty good, for little kids.

Finally it was our turn. Ms. Colman clipped on the line that would lift me up in the air. (I had practiced flying earlier in the afternoon. I have to tell you, I was a natural.)

Addie Sidney, in a white beard and red suit, rolled out onstage first. Her wheelchair was decorated with green and red streamers. A big sack stuffed with pretend presents was tied to the back of her chair. Addie let out a "Ho! Ho! Ho!" and the music started.

We trooped onstage, singing the first words of the song: "Rudolph the Red-Nosed Reindeer . . ."

It was hard to see the audience, but I peered into the darkness and finally picked out Daddy (with a video camera in front of his face) and Elizabeth and Nannie and all the big-house kids. Nearby were Mommy and Seth and Merry, my little-house nanny. I

95

was so, so happy! Both of my families were there to see me. That was a special Christmas treat.

But I had to pretend to be sad. We were singing the part about how the other reindeer would not let Rudolph join in any reindeer games. I slumped my shoulders and shuffled to the edge of the stage.

Then the part came about the foggy Christmas Eve, when Santa needed Rudolph to guide his sleigh. I pranced back to the center of the stage, and we reindeer all lined up in front of Addie. We pretended to pull the sleigh through the air.

When we got to the final line, about Rudolph going down in histoorrrrryyy, Mr. Wickersham pulled the cable attached to my harness, and I rose into the air. I was filled with the Christmas spirit. Rudolph was saving Christmas. I was Rudolph, and I was saving Christmas too, by helping the lost reindeer in my backyard. Surely Santa would see that even if I had been a little naughty and had made a few mistakes, still nobody loved Christmas more than I did.

Grinning, I gazed out over the auditorium. I soared gloriously above the crowd. The applause and cheering lifted me up. I was flying. And then I stopped waiting for a sign. I was enjoying the Christmas season. That was good enough for me.

After the show, the kids from Ms. Colman's class stood around backstage and had punch and cookies.

"You were great, Karen," said Hannie.

"Thank you. You were a good elf too. But I loved flying through the air."

Hannie leaned in close to me. "Actually, Karen," she whispered, "my cold was not that bad. I just did not want to play Rudolph. I was afraid of flying around. So really you did me a favor by taking over my part."

I was surprised. I could not believe anyone would not want to fly around attached to a harness.

"I guess we did each other favors," I said. "Which is part of what Christmas is all about." I was thinking about the *big* favor I was doing for Santa.

"Merry Christmas, Karen."

"Merry Christmas, Hannie."

I am so lucky Hannie is one of my best friends.

18

Christmas Eve

On Christmas Eve my big-house family sat around the tree and sang carols. Nannie made hot cider with cinnamon sticks. We turned off all the lights except the ones on the tree. They winked and blinked white, red, and green. The ornaments — even Charlie's New York Knicks ball — and the tinsel looked beautiful in the twinkling light. I felt warm and cozy and happy.

As a special treat, we each got to open one present early. I was surprised to remember that people in my family would give me presents too — not just Santa. I felt extra happy all over again, because I realized that having a family who loves me and would give me presents was enough to save Christmas for me.

I decided to open my present from Kristy. While everyone watched, I tore off the paper and ripped off the ribbon. "A watercolor set and a pad of paper for painting on!" I exclaimed. "Thank you, Kristy!" I gave her a big hug. "What a great present!"

"The paper is specially made for watercolors," Kristy said. She hugged me back. "Merry Christmas Eve, Karen."

"Merry Christmas Eve, everyone!" I replied. Then I was so full of Christmas spirit that I went around the room and hugged everyone, even David Michael (a person I do not hug very often).

Finally bedtime came. I went to my room and gazed out the window. The reindeer was not there. I had not seen the reindeer in several days. That must be a good sign, I decided. He must have found his way back to the North Pole in time to pull Santa's sleigh.

I got out the Karen Chart one last time. I was still deep in the naughty zone. I had made a minor comeback in the last few days, but breaking Nannie's vase outweighed any good I had done. I still felt terrible about it. I wondered if Santa would overlook the vase incident.

Probably not.

I would be lucky to get a single orange in the toe of my stocking. I could forget about candy or any real presents from Santa. But I had my family. It still felt like Christmas.

I put away the Karen Chart and climbed into bed.

By feeding the reindeer, I had probably saved Christmas for everyone but myself. I felt good about that.

I thought about Andrew asleep in the next room, waiting for Santa to come. He would be so disappointed if Santa did not make it. And there were millions of kids all over the world, just like Andrew, depending on Santa. The thought of all those children having a wonderful, happy Christmas, thanks to me, cheered me up.

I closed my eyes and started drifting off to sleep. . . .

Suddenly I heard a noise in the living room. It sounded like someone thumping around down there.

Santa! It must be Santa!

I sat bolt upright. This was my last chance. Maybe I could go downstairs and explain to Santa that I had not meant to be naughty. Breaking the vase had been an accident, and all the other things that had gone wrong had been accidents too. Could I have a second (or third, or fourth) chance?

I ducked under my bed and gathered up the newspaper that held the broken vase and the wilted flowers. As I trotted downstairs with them, I thought about what I would say.

When I got to the bottom of the stairs, I heard a voice coming from the living room. But it was not Santa's voice.

It was Nannie's. And she was saying, "I

just cannot figure out what happened to that vase. I have looked all over for it, and I cannot find it anywhere."

"That is strange," said Daddy.

"I cannot imagine what could have happened to it," said Elizabeth.

Oh, no! This was not my last chance. This was going to be my final punishment. It was what I had been dreading: having to tell my family what I had done. Yes, I could go upstairs and hide the vase again and pretend it had never happened. But that seemed like an awful thing to do on Christmas Eve.

All at once I could not hold it in any longer.

"I have it!" I cried, running into the living room. I opened up the folded newspaper and showed them the fragments of glass. "I broke it. I am sorry!"

I burst into tears.

19

Nannie's Vase?

"Karen, be careful with that broken glass," Nannie said. She took the bundle from me. "Now, tell me what happened to the vase, and why you wrapped the pieces up in a newspaper."

It all came out. I told Daddy, Elizabeth, and Nannie about my chart. I even went to my room and brought it out for them to see. I told them about trying to be good, but that everything went wrong. I told them about how I broke Nannie's grandmother's special crystal vase, and that I did not know what to do about it. I told them about Santa's lost reindeer, and how I fed it and helped save Christmas.

"I saved Christmas for everyone but me!" I wailed. "I have been so naughty, I am sure I am going to get nothing but coal and straw in my stocking."

I sobbed and sobbed.

"Come here, sweetie," said Daddy. He put his arms around me.

"Karen, the vase you broke was not my grandmother's crystal vase," Nannie said.

I stopped sobbing. "It was not?"

"No. That vase is over there in the hutch, as good as new. See? The vase you broke was just a cheap glass one from a florist," Nannie went on. "Breaking it was no big deal."

"Really?" I asked.

"No," said Nannie. "And you were not horsing around in the living room when you broke it. You were dusting. It was a simple accident. It was not being naughty."

"Oh," I said.

"However, you should have told an adult when you broke it," Daddy pointed out. "Instead of hiding the evidence. Once it was broken, there was nothing you could have done to fix it. But trying to pretend it did not happen was naughty."

I started tearing up again. "So I am still naughty!" I said. "And Santa still will not come for me this year."

Daddy patted my shoulder. "Santa will forgive a little naughtiness, Karen," he said. "He is not so harsh. I am sure that Santa knows you mean well, even if you do slip up every now and then."

"That is right," said Elizabeth. "Why, as naughty as Sam and Charlie and Kristy were when they were your age, Santa always brought them something."

"Kristy was naughty?" I asked, amazed. I could believe Sam and Charlie were naughty, but Kristy?

"They had their moments," Elizabeth

said. "But overall, they were good kids, just like you. And that is what matters to Santa. Not a couple of slipups."

"I am pretty sure you will get something from Santa," Daddy said. He kissed my cheek. "Now run along and go to bed. You have a big day tomorrow."

"Okay, Daddy," I said. I cannot tell you how relieved I felt. It was as if a huge brick had been taken off my chest. All these weeks I had been so worried about the vase, and now I felt free again. My family had forgiven me. I knew that Santa would forgive me too. "Yippee!" I said softly, padding my way upstairs.

On my way up, I ran into Charlie, coming down.

"Hey, Karen," he said. He glanced down at his watch. "Past your bedtime, isn't it?"

I nodded. "I had something important to talk about with the grown-ups," I said. "Good night."

"Oh, Karen," said Charlie. "I wanted to

tell you that I think your reindeer got back to the North Pole safely."

I stopped. "Really? How do you know?"

Charlie smiled. "Let's just say I have some inside information. I have a feeling that Santa is very grateful for the help you gave his reindeer."

"Gosh," I said, wide-eyed. "Well, good night again, Charlie."

"Good night, Karen. And Merry Christmas."

Merry Christmas!

My eyes popped open. I looked at my clock. Six twenty-seven! I had to wait three more minutes before rushing downstairs to see if Santa had brought me anything.

I was so nervous and excited, I could hardly lie still. My toes wiggled. My knees wiggled. My bottom wiggled. I wiggled all over and thrashed my head around on my pillow.

I glanced at my clock. Six twenty-eight.

Finally, a long one hundred and twenty seconds later, six-thirty came.

I leaped out of bed and raced into the hallway. David Michael and Andrew were there too, in their pajamas. The three of us dashed downstairs.

This was the moment of truth. Now I would find out whether my reindeer had made it back to the North Pole in time to pull the sleigh. And I would find out whether I was on Santa's "naughty" list or his "nice" one.

All sorts of packages lay scattered beneath the tree. Seven full stockings — one each for Sam, Charlie, Kristy, David Michael, Andrew, Emily Michelle, and me — hung from the mantelpiece.

"Hooray!" I cried. "Santa came!"

I ran to the Christmas tree and checked the labels. "To David Michael, from Santa Claus," read the first one I checked. "To Kristy, from Santa," read the next.

Then: "To Karen, from Santa Claus"!

I threw my arms in the air and shouted, "Yea! Santa brought me something! Merry Christmas!"

"Merry Christmas, Karen," said Daddy.

I turned around. There were Daddy, Elizabeth, and Nannie in their bathrobes.

"Merry Christmas!" I said again. I reached into my stocking. No coal! No straw! I pulled out a candy cane. A chocolate Santa. A marzipan pig. A hair ribbon, brand-new crayons, a bracelet. It was a Christmas miracle.

My family was talking and laughing. David Michael blew on a harmonica. Emily Michelle shook a snow globe. I thought about my reindeer.

I reached into my stocking again and pulled out a miniature book, a roll of butterscotch Life Savers, an egg of Silly Putty. At last only one thing was left. Far down in the toe of my stocking was a small box. It was wrapped in shiny paper. I stared at it. Inside was a tiny silver charm in the shape of a reindeer. Under the charm lay a folded piece of paper.

My heart began to pound.

I unfolded the paper. Written in blue ink was a note to me:

Dear Karen,
   Thank you for taking such good care of Blitzen. I found him safe and sound.
      Have a Merry Christmas!
         Love,
         Santa Claus

Oh, my gosh. A note from Santa Claus himself! I stared around at my family, who were opening their presents and talking and laughing and hugging. The biggest Christmas present ever had just happened, and they didn't even know about it. Carefully I folded the note and slipped it into my robe pocket. I would treasure it forever.

But, as it turned out, I would never see my reindeer again.

Merry Christmas!

Love, Karen.

L. GODWIN

About the Author

ANN M. MARTIN lives in New York City and loves animals, especially cats. She has two cats of her own, Gussie and Woody.

Other books by Ann M. Martin that you might enjoy are *Stage Fright*; *Me and Katie (the Pest)*; and the books in *The Baby-sitters Club* series.

Ann likes ice cream and *I Love Lucy*. And she has her own little sister, whose name is Jane.

Little Sister

Don't miss #117

KAREN'S MISTAKE

"Ten! Nine! Eight! Seven! Six! Five! Four! Three! Two! One! Happy new year!" we all shouted.

Horns blew. Our homemade confetti went flying in the air.

I was jumping up and down with Nancy when I saw Hannie looking over at us. I knew right then that I did not want to start the new year being mad at my friend. I held out my hand for Hannie to join us.

The Three Musketeers were jumping up and down together. While I was jumping up, I saw something that made my eyes open wide.

I saw Nannie being kissed on the cheek by Mr. English!

BABY-SITTERS™

Little Sister

by Ann M. Martin
author of The Baby-sitters Club®

More Titles... ➡

☑ MQ69188-0 #80	**Karen's Christmas Tree**	$2.99
☐ MQ69189-9 #81	**Karen's Accident**	$2.99
☐ MQ69190-2 #82	**Karen's Secret Valentine**	$3.50
☐ MQ69191-0 #83	**Karen's Bunny**	$3.50
☐ MQ69192-9 #84	**Karen's Big Job**	$3.50
☐ MQ69193-7 #85	**Karen's Treasure**	$3.50
☐ MQ69194-5 #86	**Karen's Telephone Trouble**	$3.50
☐ MQ06585-8 #87	**Karen's Pony Camp**	$3.50
☐ MQ06586-6 #88	**Karen's Puppet Show**	$3.50
☐ MQ06587-4 #89	**Karen's Unicorn**	$3.50
☐ MQ06588-2 #90	**Karen's Haunted House**	$3.50
☐ MQ06589-0 #91	**Karen's Pilgrim**	$3.50
☐ MQ06590-4 #92	**Karen's Sleigh Ride**	$3.50
☐ MQ06591-2 #93	**Karen's Cooking Contest**	$3.50
☐ MQ06592-0 #94	**Karen's Snow Princess**	$3.50
☐ MQ06593-9 #95	**Karen's Promise**	$3.50
☐ MQ06594-7 #96	**Karen's Big Move**	$3.50
☐ MQ06595-5 #97	**Karen's Paper Route**	$3.50
☐ MQ06596-3 #98	**Karen's Fishing Trip**	$3.50
☐ MQ49760-X #99	**Karen's Big City Mystery**	$3.50
☐ MQ50051-1 #100	**Karen's Book**	$3.50
☐ MQ50053-8 #101	**Karen's Chain Letter**	$3.50
☐ MQ50054-6 #102	**Karen's Black Cat**	$3.50
☐ MQ50055-4 #103	**Karen's Movie Star**	$3.99
☐ MQ50056-2 #104	**Karen's Christmas Carol**	$3.99
☐ MQ50057-0 #105	**Karen's Nanny**	$3.99
☐ MQ50058-9 #106	**Karen's President**	$3.99
☐ MQ50059-7 #107	**Karen's Copycat**	$3.99
☐ MQ43647-3	**Karen's Wish Super Special #1**	$3.25
☐ MQ44834-X	**Karen's Plane Trip Super Special #2**	$3.25
☐ MQ44827-7	**Karen's Mystery Super Special #3**	$3.25
☐ MQ45644-X	**Karen, Hannie, and Nancy**	
	The Three Musketeers Super Special #4	$2.95
☐ MQ45649-0	**Karen's Baby Super Special #5**	$3.50
☑ MQ46911-8	**Karen's Campout Super Special #6**	$3.25
☐ MQ55407-7	**BSLS Jump Rope Pack**	$5.99
☐ MQ73914-X	**BSLS Playground Games Pack**	$5.99
☐ MQ89735-7	**BSLS Photo Scrapbook Book and Camera Pack**	$9.99
☐ MQ47677-7	**BSLS School Scrapbook**	$2.95
☐ MQ13801-4	**Baby-sitters Little Sister Laugh Pack**	$6.99
☐ MQ26497-2	**Karen's Summer Fill-In Book**	$2.95

Available wherever you buy books, or use this order form.

Scholastic Inc., P.O. Box 7502, Jefferson City, MO 65102

Please send me the books I have checked above. I am enclosing
$_____
(please add $2.00 to cover shipping and handling). Send check or money order — no cash or C.O.Ds please.

Name_____ Birthdate_____

Address_____

City_____ State/Zip_____

Please allow four to six weeks for delivery. Offer good in U.S.A. only. Sorry, mail orders are not available to residents of Canada. Prices subject to change.   BSLS998